# MUDDY WATERS
# MIDSUMMER MILLY

I'M ONLY SMALL, AND SOMETIMES TINY. I'M ON EVERY PAGE, CAN YOU FIND ME?

Working hard on the Ship Canal is what Milly likes best. She enjoys nothing more than delivering her precious cargo to all the quays and wharfs in her home city of Manchester. With her cheery smile and happy 'toot toot', she is welcomed wherever she goes. Even the grumpiest and rudest of boats love Milly, including Cedric the Dredger at Thrupp Wharf. This is where Milly was about to make a very special journey.

Despite staying cheerful, she had been struggling with her loads for some time. Perhaps a trip to see Muddy Waters is what I need to pick me up she thought, as she set off on her journey. The Thrupp boats were very excited about her visit.

'It's about time we had a working boat in the wharf,' said Cedric, looking hard at Jolly Boatman.

'I am a working boat,' said Jolly indignantly.

'Pah! You've never done a hard day's work in your life,' snorted Cedric, as he headed off to see his close friend Coal Face.

Jolly took no notice because Muddy Waters had let him into a sad secret. Milly was heading south, not just to deliver her cargo, but to call in on Old Badger. Her hull was beginning to crumble and flake and it was making her feel very sick and weary.

As all narrowboats know, a visit to Old Badger at Stoke Bruerne is often all that's needed to put things right. Muddy Waters was determined to get Milly there as soon as she could manage it.

'What's wrong with Milly's hull?' asked Jolly quietly, not wanting the others to hear.

'It's a little complicated…' replied Muddy in a whisper, 'but when she was put together the builders used the wood from one of the older boats and some from new timber. Unfortunately, the different woods reacted badly with one another, and this means Milly has had to fight hard most days to stay afloat.'

'We'll go and see Old Badger in his dry dock. He's seen this kind of thing before. He'll know what to do,' Muddy added confidently.

The next day Milly puttered merrily into Thrupp Wharf where the warmest of welcomes awaited her. Everyone fussed and bothered around her and wanted to hear all about her adventurous voyage, but Muddy Waters gently nudged her over to a quiet berth to give her time to rest.

'Such long journeys are always a little tiring,' he said knowingly. 'They certainly are,' agreed Milly as she began to relax and rest her exhausted hull. 'I am so glad to have delivered my cargo and to be here with you all. Are we off to see Old Badger tomorrow?' she asked.

'We can go whenever you are ready,' replied Muddy gently. In his heart he wanted her to go as soon as she was able. He could see she was uncomfortable and not at all her usual happy self.

Jolly puttered quietly over to where Milly was berthed and greeted her excitedly. 'I've heard so much about you,' he said, 'and I know you have a wooden hull. I hope to have one soon.' Milly interrupted Jolly. 'I wouldn't rush for a new hull just yet, Jolly,' she said gently.

'But we all know you wooden boats are soooooooooo special,' said Jolly. 'Perhaps a little too special,' said a voice from behind. It was Muddy Waters. 'You'll have plenty of time for chatter on our journey up to Stoke Bruerne tomorrow. Let's just leave Milly to get a good night's rest.'

Arriving at Old Badger's dry dock in Stoke Bruerne took all of the puff out of Milly. She was very tired as she moored alongside some of the other boats at the wharf. She hardly noticed that there were many other bright and colourful boats around, and that the wharf was covered in flags and bunting. But Jolly had noticed and he pestered Muddy Waters into telling him what was going on.

'Today is Midsummer's Day which is a very special day for all canal boats, especially here in Stoke Bruerne,' said Muddy grandly.

'Of course,' said Jolly as he remembered the stories of the nearby enchanted tunnel. Were the tales about the magical Old World through the tunnel really true he wondered, or was it just a tale told to young narrowboats?

Old Badger seemed to know what Jolly was thinking when he announced, 'Only very special boats get to go through the tunnel on this magical day, Jolly. Do you think you deserve to be one of those boats?'

Jolly frowned and thought long and hard. He so desperately wanted to see the Old World, and to meet the special horses, but as he glanced over at Milly he could see she was still very weary. 'I think Milly should go,' he said, and she gave him a tired smile and wink of thanks. Old Badger and Muddy Waters exchanged a knowing nod and agreed.

'You can come with us too, Jolly, as you've been so thoughtful, but we must hurry as we have to be back before the end of the day,' said Muddy.

Milly was too tired to go much further under her own steam, so Jolly and Muddy Waters gently guided her along. As they entered the mouth of the tunnel it became very dark and quiet as all of the engines were cut. A mysterious current tickled their hulls and pulled them further in.

The tunnel was so long it was hard to see if there was any light at the other end. Strange and unfamiliar noises could be heard up ahead. Jolly and Milly were quite frightened and wanted to turn back. Muddy Waters had been through many times before. He whispered that they would soon be there and to be brave.

Slowly the boats saw a bright light appear in front of them and they realised that they were through. Jolly and Milly went to fire up their engines but soon found they wouldn't work. Muddy Waters, already roped to the two younger boats, drifted over to the near embankment where a fine shire horse was waiting for him.

'Hello, Muddy, it's a long time since we've seen you here. Who are your handsome young friends?' The two young boats were amazed to see such a powerful creature talking and that it seemed to know Muddy Waters so well.

Milly began to look and feel very much like her old self. All of the aches and pains of her journey had gone. She could feel the cracks in her hull healing. She loved to see the other wooden boats around her all appearing to be like her, bright, shiny and new. She even thought that Jolly had taken on a new and very impressive look.

'Let's see if we can find some of my friends to tow these fine-looking boats further into the Old World,' said the shire horse. 'And you and I can catch up on past times, Muddy,' he added.

Milly and Jolly had a wonderful time learning how to work with the horses and how to get along the canal without an engine, although it did take some getting used to. Milly's horse explained how important it was that they learned to look after each other and understand the ways of the water. Milly was enjoying herself so much that she hadn't noticed time quickly passing by.

Finding Milly and Jolly much further down the canal than he had expected, Muddy Waters explained that they really must move quickly if they were not to remain in the Old World for another year.

'If we don't make it back through the tunnel before sunset we'll be stuck here,' he said gravely.

Jolly and Milly's horses both knew how serious this was and took up the strain on their ropes, pulling their boats swiftly along the canal towards the tunnel. Jolly found himself in a panic at the thought of not getting back to Thrupp and he did all he could to move rapidly through the water.

'Come on, we're nearly there,' called Muddy Waters. 'Not much further.' There was a little anxiety in his voice as he could see the sun going down over the horizon.

Milly was watching the two Thrupp boats dashing towards the tunnel entrance but she tugged on her rope and asked her horse to slow down. Knowing what was on her mind, the old horse eased up to a steady walk and gave her a nod of approval.

Jolly glanced back to see Milly drifting further away. He had slipped his rope and was now in the mouth of the tunnel. 'She's not going to make it, Muddy,' he cried, as the darkness of the entrance covered him over.

'She's chosen to stay, my boy,' said Muddy, adding, 'She's happy now, and her pains have gone. One day we'll be back in the Old World and perhaps we'll see her then.'

As the two Thrupp boats disappeared, Milly smiled and shouted a happy goodbye to them. Her horse turned her around and led her towards her new moorings and her new home in the Old World.

# Who is Muddy Waters?

Muddy Waters is no ordinary narrowboat as you'll discover in this exciting new series of stories. Set in well known and loved locations throughout Britain's beautiful waterways, you'll soon become familiar with such colourful characters as Dizzy Spells, Cedric, Dawn Chorus, Dudley and the rest of Muddy's buddies. Muddy invites you to find out so much more at

## www.muddywaters.org.uk

### Glossary

**Cargo:** things like wood and coal carried from place to place by the boats

**Quay:** a platform by or in water for loading and unloading boats

**Wharf:** a place where boats can stop to load and unload their cargo and where they can stay for a while

**Narrowboat:** a canal boat less than 2.1 metres wide that is steered with a tiller, not a wheel

**Hull:** the main part of a boat, including the bottom, sides and deck

**Dry dock:** a dock is a place on the wharf where boats are repaired and where they load and unload cargo. A Dry dock is one which has been drained of water, so that the hull is kept dry

**Berth:** a special place at a wharf where boats can rest

**Mooring:** a space where the boats can stop and be attached to the canal bank with a rope

**Embankment:** a wall or bank built to prevent flooding by a river or canal

# Other Titles Available...

Poppy at the Boat Show

Pearly's Welcome to London

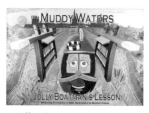

Jolly Boatman's Lesson

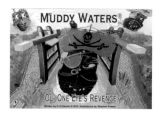

Ol' One Eye's Revenge

## Stay **SAFE** near water -
## **S**tay **A**way **F**rom the **E**dge

wild over waterways

**Go Wild Over Waterways -** find games, learning and fun things to do at www.wow4water.net

MANCHESTER

BIRMINGHAM ·

Milly

STOKE BRUERNE

THRUPP

OXFORD

BRISTOL

· READING ·